Scruffy Ted

Story written by Gill Munton
Illustrated by Tim Archbold

Speed Sounds

Consonants *Ask children to say the sounds.*

f	l	m	n	r	s	v	z	sh	(th)	(ng)
(ff)	(ll)		nn		ss	(ve)	zz			(nk)
	(le)		kn				s			

b	c	d	g	h	j	p	qu	t	w	x	y	(ch)
bb	k	dd	gg			pp		(tt)	wh			tch
	(ck)											

Each box contains one sound but sometimes more than one grapheme.
*Focus graphemes for this story are **circled**.*

Vowels

Ask children to say the sounds in and out of order.

a	e ea	i	o	u	ay	ee y	igh	ow
at	hen	in	on	up	day	see	high	blow

oo	oo	ar	or	air	ir	ou	oy
zoo	look	car	for	fair	whirl	shout	boy

Story Green Words

Ask children to read the words first in Fred Talk and then say the word.

Ann   Gran   Finn   Panda Peg   Hissy Hetty

Jack-in-a-box   Scruffy Ted   check   doll   rag

Ask children to say the syllables and then read the whole word.

cudd|le   spag|hett|i   jim|jams   tink|ly

pupp|y   fluff|y

Ask children to read the root first and then the whole word with the suffix.

jump → jumping   tuck → tucked

6

Red Words

Ask children to practise reading the words across the rows, down the columns and in and out of order clearly and quickly.

all	my	like*	I've
the	are	said	go
you	your	are	be
to	me	of	he

*Red Word in this book only.

Scruffy Ted

Ann

This doll is Ann

(I got Ann from my gran).

The fluffy cat is Finn

(I can put my jimjams in).

Finn

I've got Panda Peg as well

(I can ring the tinkly bell).

Ting

The rag doll is Hissy Hetty
(long legs like spaghetti).

The puppy dog is Spot
(I cuddle him such a lot).

This is jumping Jack-in-the-box
(in his red and black check socks).

And this is Scruffy Ted
(the ted tucked up in bed).

kiss kiss

I cuddle all the rest ...

but Scruffy Ted's the best!

Questions to talk about

Ask children to TTYP for each question using 'Fastest finger' (FF) or 'Have a think' (HaT).

p.8   (FF)   Who gave Meg her doll?

p.9   (FF)   Where does Meg keep her jimjams?

p.10 (FF)   What do Hissy Hetty's legs remind Meg of?

p.11 (FF)   What does the Jack-in-the-box do?

p.12 (HaT) Why do you think Scruffy Ted is called Scruffy Ted?

p.13 (FF)   Which toys does Meg cuddle?